GUS THE BEAR,

The Flying Cat,

AND the

Lovesick **MOOSE**

TWENTY **REAL LIFE**
ANIMAL STORIES

Books by Daniel Cohen

THE GHOSTS OF WAR
PHANTOM ANIMALS
PHONE CALL FROM A GHOST: Strange Tales from
   Modern America
REAL GHOSTS
THE WORLD'S MOST FAMOUS GHOSTS
GHOSTLY TALES OF LOVE AND REVENGE

Available from MINSTREL Books

GUS THE BEAR,
The Flying Cat,
and the
Lovesick MOOSE

TWENTY **REAL LIFE** ANIMAL STORIES

Daniel Cohen

A MINSTREL® BOOK

Published by POCKET BOOKS
New York   London   Toronto   Sydney   Tokyo   Singapore

A MINSTREL PAPERBACK *Original*

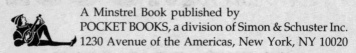

A Minstrel Book published by
POCKET BOOKS, a division of Simon & Schuster Inc.
1230 Avenue of the Americas, New York, NY 10020

Copyright © 1995 by Daniel Cohen

All rights reserved, including the right to reproduce
this book or portions thereof in any form whatsoever.
For information address Pocket Books, 1230 Avenue
of the Americas, New York, NY 10020

ISBN: 0-671-53624-9

First Minstrel Books printing December 1995

10 9 8 7 6 5 4 3 2 1

A MINSTREL BOOK and colophon are registered trademarks of
Simon & Schuster Inc.

Front cover photo credits: top left Reuters/Bettmann; top right
AP; bottom Larry Carrara. Back cover photo by AP/Wide World.

Printed in the U.S.A.

In memory of Tom Aylesworth

Contents

GUS THE BEAR,

The Flying Cat,
And the
Lovesick MOOSE

TWENTY **REAL LIFE**
ANIMAL STORIES

Introduction

In the News

There was once this polar bear named Gus. He just kept swimming around his pool at the Central Park Zoo in New York.

And there was once this cat, Tabitha, that got lost in the cargo hold of a 747 jet and was flown all over the country.

And don't forget the Vermont moose that fell in love with a cow named Jessica.

How about the three whales that got stuck in the ice off the coast of Alaska and had reporters from all over the world rushing up to one of the coldest places on earth?

There was even this tankful of humble newts at the Philadelphia Zoo.

These animals, and others you will meet in this book, are creatures whose stories have somehow caught the public's attention. They have, so to speak, risen above the herd. They are animals in the news.

1

Gus the Bear

This is a story that could happen only in New York.

Once upon a time, in the Central Park Zoo, right in the middle of Manhattan there was this confused polar bear.

Gus, a 700-pound polar bear, lived (and still lives) in a large slate-gray enclosure of real and fake rock. He shares his space with two female polar bears named Lily and Ida.

In the midst of a sweltering New York summer in 1994, Lily and Ida were doing the usual things that captive polar bears do when the temperature tops 90 degrees. They lay on their backs, scratched, slept, and watched the people watching them. Occasionally they took a dip in the enclosure's large, deep pool. They appeared happy with life.

Gus was different. Every morning he was in the pool. He would push off from the rock with his hind paws and take a couple of strokes on his back to the other side. Then he would dive underwater and pass the viewing window, leaving a trail of bubbles. And when he completed the lap, he would do it over again in exactly the same pattern, right down to the way his tongue flicked across his black lips. He would swim like a bear on a mission for hours on end.

Regular visitors to the zoo noticed Gus's strange behavior, and one day, a reporter for the New York newspaper *Newsday* noticed it as well. The newspaper put Gus and his strange behavior on the front page.

Now unfortunately, Gus's problem is not all that uncommon among zoo animals. Some animals fall into this sort of repetitive behavior when they are kept in small cages with nothing to do. A tiger will pace back and forth in exactly the same pattern day after day. An elephant will shift endlessly from one foot to another.

Zoos are well aware of the problem and the better ones try to correct it by giving animals larger living spaces and more things to do. The Central Park Zoo had recently been renovated at a cost of $38 million. Gus's enclosure was the best money could buy for polar bears. There was the pool, there were rocks to climb on, there were toys to play with, and a lot of attention from both the zookeepers and the public. The other bears seemed to like it fine. But not Gus.

It wasn't that Gus was longing for the Arctic and hunting seals across the ice floes. Gus was born in the Toledo Zoo in Ohio. He didn't know anything about ice floes or seal hunts. He had been a perfectly normal and happy cub, and showed no signs of this behavior until he moved to New York.

As soon as the story of Gus hit the press, he became famous. New Yorkers who were feeling hot, stressed out, trapped, and more than a little

Gus the bear licks peanut butter off a beach ball. Putting Gus's favorite foods in tricky places is part of his therapy.

crazy themselves took the confused polar bear to their hearts.

He was featured on the evening TV news. David Letterman, the late-night talk show host, told Gus the bear jokes. Radio stations from all over the world called the Central Park Zoo for information on Gus's condition. *The New York Times*, which usually has editorials about government and world affairs, wrote one about Gus. Some of the animal rights organizations, which don't like zoos anyway, took up the cause of Gus. They told people to boycott all zoos.

In response to all the publicity and the criticism, the zoo hired an animal psychiatrist. He was Tim Desmond, an animal behavior expert who trained the killer whale in the popular film *Free Willy*. Desmond's fee for helping Gus was $25,000. This made Gus even more famous.

After watching Gus for a while, Desmond concluded that there was nothing physically wrong with the bear. He wasn't crazy either. He was just hot and bored. Or, as Desmond put it, he wasn't "getting all the behavioral opportunities he needs."

The expert's remedy was give Gus more to do. Now the bear has to work for his food. For example, his afternoon serving of peanut butter is no longer just smeared on a rock, where he can lick it off without any effort. Now the peanut butter is put in a bucket, which is tossed into the pool. Gus has to dive for it. This is just one of the ways he retrieves his afternoon snack.

The zookeepers don't just throw him fish anymore, either. Sometimes the fish are frozen inside a 25-pound block of ice. Gus has to tear away at the ice with his claws to get his meal. Some of his other food is hidden in the rocks and caves of his space. A few of his favorite toys are hidden there, too. There are now more challenges in Gus's daily life.

As a result, Gus is spending less time in the pool and more time doing other things. But he's not totally "cured" and probably never will be. He is going to have to receive special attention for the rest of his life.

Why Gus became bored while the other polar

bears living under exactly the same conditions have not is still a mystery. But there is no mystery about why Gus the bear became famous. "Gus has struck some sort of a chord," said a spokeswoman for the zoo. "It is a problem people relate to."

Especially New Yorkers.

2

The Flying Cat

Have you ever seen one of those TV airline ads that refers to "frequent fliers"? A frequent flier is someone who flies a lot. Any airline would like to keep that person's business. So many airlines will reward such travelers with "frequent flier miles," which allow people to fly for free or at reduced rates. The more you fly, the more you can fly free.

Tabitha, a three-year-old domestic shorthair cat, could probably apply for lots of these "frequent flier" miles on Tower Air. But she wouldn't want them. She has done enough flying for nine lives.

On June 30, 1994, Tabitha was making a cat's standard flight from New York to Los Angeles. She was in a pet carrier placed in the cargo hold of a Tower Airlines 747 jet. Her owner, Carol Ann Timmel, was moving to Los Angeles to pursue an acting career.

Somehow—no one knows how—Tabitha got out of her carrier and escaped into the plane's vast cargo hold. Tabitha was traveling with her "sister cat" Pandora in the same carrier. (Pandora, who was not true to her name, stayed in the box.)

When Carol Ann got the cat carrier at the end of the flight, there was only one cat in it. She was both heartbroken and angry. She knew her cat was somewhere on the plane, and she demanded that the airline find the cat.

The airline was willing to look for Tabitha, so long as the plane was on the ground. But airplanes are very expensive pieces of equipment, and Tower Air could not afford to ground the plane until the cat was found.

And so began Tabitha's career as a frequent flier. For the next 12 days, the 747 jet flew regularly between New York and Los Angeles with side trips to Miami, Florida, and San Juan, Puerto Rico. All in all, it logged some 30,000 flying miles.

When the plane was not actually in the air, about 12 to 14 hours every day, airline personnel searched the cargo hold for Tabitha. The searches were unsuccessful. The cargo hold itself is about the size of two football fields, with plenty of places for a cat to hide. Cats are wonderful at hiding.

In the meantime, the story of the cat trapped in an airplane attracted the attention of reporters in both New York and Los Angeles. It also attracted the attention of a number of animal rights organizations. Pesky Critters, a group that rescues animals, joined the search with volunteers from other organizations every time the plane landed. A variety of cat traps baited with tuna and other feline favorites were scattered about the cargo hold. A psychic was even called in to find the cat's hiding place. Nothing worked.

The Flying Cat

Tabitha was in there somewhere, but for her own reasons, she was not about to reveal her hiding place.

Things got a bit tense. Carol Ann wanted to have the plane grounded and searched until Tabitha was found. Her lawyer was even threatening to go to court to force the airline to ground the plane.

Tower Air responded by saying it was doing everything it could, short of taking the aircraft out of service. The airline even said that it would set a time so Carol Ann and animal rescue professionals could search for the cat with minicameras and other high-tech equipment. The airline was going to pay for the search, which would have been expensive. But at the last minute, an airline spokesman said, Carol Ann backed out, citing a previous engagement.

Over 12 days, 100 airline workers looked for Tabitha for some 1,000 hours, according to the airline. They believed that it was the most thorough and expensive search for a pet in history. Just how much all of this cost no one knew.

Carol Ann Timmel is reunited with Tabitha the flying cat.

The Flying Cat

Finally, when the plane touched down at Kennedy Airport at midnight on July 11, it was moved to an isolated spot where it was quiet, so that faint cat sounds could be heard. A New York Supreme Court judge had ordered the plane grounded for a 24-hour search by Carol Ann and a group of airline employees.

Some nine hours into the search, Carol Ann heard a rustling sound below the floor of the passenger compartment.

Then there was what Carol Ann called "this wondrous meow." Her reaction: "I just lost it."

Carol Ann began calling the cat's name, and Tabitha responded. This allowed searchers to get a fix on the cat's location. Mechanics removed an inspection hatch and spotted the stowaway in a 7-inch-high, 60-foot-long space. Psychic Christa Carol claimed that she had pointed to the spot where Tabitha was later found. But the psychic wasn't part of the team that finally rescued the cat.

Tabitha was captured and immediately rushed to the New York office of veterinarian Dr. Keith Manning. Dr. Manning pronounced

Tabitha thirsty, hungry, but otherwise fit. She had lost about 2 pounds during her time on the plane.

Like her ordeal, Tabitha's rescue was big news. *The New York Times* even had an editorial about the rescue. It ended with the words, "Nine hours later, she exited. With Tabitha. And the cheers of all cat lovers."

Tower Air, which had been getting a lot of bad publicity, as well as losing a lot of money, was relieved. "Fortunately, and somewhat miraculously, Tabitha has been found and returned to her owner in good health. And when all is said and done, this was the only goal that we all shared," wrote airline Vice President L. Nick Lacey.

The next day Carol Ann and her cat made one more flight from New York to Los Angeles. It was in first class, and Tabitha had a seat right next to her owner. No more time in the cargo hold for her.

Donald David, Carol Ann's lawyer, was asked if Tabitha would apply for frequent flier miles. He said that it was "irrelevant, because the cat doesn't intend to fly anymore, other than to go home to California."

Well, perhaps not, but a few weeks later lawyer David reported that the cat was considering "two offers for books and three for movies." Those book promotion tours usually involve a lot of flying.

3

The Lovesick Moose

Let us get one thing very clear right at the start. To most of us who have never met a moose, it is a big, funny-looking animal. With its enormous antlers and long snout, it looks like something out of a cartoon. In fact, the moose is often used in cartoons.

In the real world, however, the moose is anything but funny. They are huge animals. Adult males stand over 6 feet tall from the ground to the shoulders and can weigh up to 900 pounds. The antlers are used by a male moose, or bull moose, to threaten and fight off rivals during the mating season. They can be dangerous weapons.

Yet despite its size, the moose is very secretive and shy. Even people who live in areas where there are wild moose rarely—if ever—see one. The moose that feels threatened can and will kill a person.

So no one expects to see a moose in a backyard. Not even when a person lives in moose country.

That is why Larry Carrara was so surprised one Sunday morning in October, 1986, when he found a moose standing just beyond a low wire fence around a cow pasture near his farmhouse in Shrewsbury, Vermont. The moose wasn't exactly in his backyard. But it was close.

He called his wife Lila out to look. Larry had seen moose before in the deep woods. Lila had never seen one in the wild. She was impressed. It was so big! They watched the moose for half an hour, expecting that any moment it would bolt into the woods and disappear. But it didn't.

The moose was a large male. That was easy to tell because it had antlers. Female moose don't have antlers. Every spring, the adult bull moose begin to grow a new set of antlers. By the fall, the antlers are ready for use in battles against other males during the mating season.

After a while Larry quietly went back to the house to get his camera. He even brought his children out to see the moose. It didn't seem very disturbed by the human activity. It continued to browse the twigs and bark of balsam trees. This is the usual moose food. After a few hours, it disappeared for a short time. It reappeared, walking down an old logging trail right into the pasture where three cows were grazing. The moose stepped easily over the electrified wire that was strung about 18 inches off the ground. A moose has very long legs. The wire was the only fence around the cow pasture. Generally, it is the only fence that is needed, because cows don't like to jump.

Two of the cows were terrified, and did jump the electrified fence to get away from the newcomer. The third cow, a rather placid brown and white Hereford named Jessica, chose not to run. She watched the moose suspiciously, but otherwise kept on grazing.

The moose began following Jessica around the

pasture. When it got too close, she would move away. This went on for hours. It was the mating season, and clearly this moose was in love.

When Larry and Lila finally went in for dinner that evening, they could still see the moose following Jessica around in the fading light. They thought that they had been lucky enough to see a unique but temporary sight. Surely by morning the moose would be gone.

But it wasn't. As Larry went out into the pasture the next morning to bring Jessica a pail of grain, he found himself face to face with the moose. He put down the pail and carefully backed away. With a moose, you can't be too careful.

The second day between the moose and the cow was very much like the first. It followed Jessica around. She mostly avoided the moose, but did not run away. Sometimes it even got close enough to put its head on her back and nuzzle her.

That evening Larry phoned the state game warden. He wanted the warden to come by the next morning to look at the moose. He wanted to be sure the moose wasn't sick, and wouldn't harm the other animals.

The game warden, Don Gallus, came by the next morning. The moose was still there. From the size of its antlers, Gallus thought that this moose was about 2½ years old. It must have weighed 700 pounds. He watched it for several hours. It seemed to be in perfect health. The only thing odd about its behavior was that it allowed people to get quite close to it. And, of course, its attachment to Jessica the cow.

The game warden had a theory about that. During the mating season the male moose looks for a female moose or moose cow that is willing to accept it. This moose apparently couldn't find one. He wandered out of the deep woods and found the Hereford. This cow didn't run away, so the moose decided to stick around. The game warden said, ''We know that moose have excellent hearing and a very good sense of smell. We also know that their vision is poor. I guess this proves it.''

During the mating season, a bull moose will normally stay with a moose cow for about 10

The odd couple, Jessica the cow and her lovesick admirer the moose.

(Vyto Starinskas/Rutland Herald.)

days. This bull moose did not seem very aggressive or in any way dangerous, so long as it did not feel threatened. The game warden figured that it might hang around Jessica for another week or so, then retreat into the deep woods to resume its solitary life.

The moose kept following Jessica. Sometimes when she got tired of it, she would go and lie down under a tree. The branches were so low that it couldn't follow without getting its antlers caught. It would stand a few feet away, staring at her.

In addition to following Jessica, the moose, whom Larry began calling Josh, did the usual moose things. It scraped its antlers on bushes, bellowed occasionally, and, of course, spent a lot of time browsing.

Every morning when Larry got up and went down to the pasture, he expected that Josh would be gone. But every morning the moose was still there. Sometimes the moose would even walk over to him and make soft blowing noises.

A week went by. And then another. Still the moose didn't leave. Now it was really unusual.

First the neighbors began to visit for a look. And as word spread, reporters came and then television crews. School children were bused in to see the moose and the cow. Then tourists began to appear.

Soon everybody in the country knew about what was being called The Lovesick Moose, The Odd Couple, or The Shrewsbury Moose.

The crowds, at first just a few people, then hundreds and sometimes thousands at a time, didn't usually bother the normally solitary and aggressive animal. Once, however, the moose felt trapped by a crowd and it charged. People scattered in all directions, and the moose stopped before hurting anyone. After that, it calmed down and there was no more trouble.

November 15 was the start of hunting season. It is illegal to hunt moose in Vermont in any season. But Larry was still worried. He posted No Hunting signs all around his property. On that day, the moose changed its routine. It crossed the road and moved into the pasture nearest the house. This is where all the other cattle except Jessica had gathered since Josh arrived. Jessica remained in her pasture.

The other cows were still afraid of the moose and ran every time it approached them. By late afternoon, it had given up trying to get close to the other cows. After Larry cleared some of the onlookers from the road, the moose again crossed over to the pasture where Jessica was placidly eating hay.

The next day the moose was back in the field with the other cattle, but this time Jessica had followed him. She got over one fence, but couldn't get over the other. Larry opened a gate for her. She immediately walked over to the moose and nuzzled it. It pushed some hay toward her and rested its head on her back while she ate.

By now the other cattle had become used to the moose. They didn't run away anymore. They even let it herd them around. One of the young bulls even seemed to admire the moose. He began to follow the moose around.

It was winter in Vermont now, and snow covered the ground. The moose began to spend more time out of the pasture and in the woods. Josh didn't eat the hay or other food put out for the cattle, and it had probably eaten all the twigs and shoots nearby. It had widened its range in search of food. But every morning Josh was back. When the cattle lay down to rest, the moose was among them. He always found a spot near Jessica.

By New Year's Eve the moose had been on the Carrara farm for 68 days. The moose and the cow had become world famous. Some 70,000 people had traveled up the narrow country road to see them. One Saturday alone there were 4,000 visitors. Cards, letters, poems, and songs were arriving from places as far away as Australia.

The moose continued to follow its usual routine. But at the start of the second week in January, when it returned from the woods, one of its antlers was missing. It was natural. A moose always loses its antlers and begins to grow a new set in the spring. But it was a sign of change.

A few days later Larry got up as usual and looked for Josh, but Josh was gone. Larry hoped it would return, but it didn't. A little later that day Lila received a phone call from a neighbor. The moose had walked right through her barnyard that morning. Now both antlers were missing. The moose seemed to be in a hurry. And it seemed to know where it was going.

It never returned to the Carrara farm, although it had stayed an incredible 76 days.

As for Jessica, she remained her old placid, easygoing self. She still stayed a little apart from the other cattle, as if she knew she was special.

If she misses her moose, she isn't saying.

4

A Very Small Dog
Story

It is illegal to bring a dog on a New York City subway train unless the dog is a seeing-eye dog or the dog is very small and can be carried in a closed container and does not bother other passengers.

Tetley is a chihuahua who weighs about 4 pounds, and can easily be carried in a zipped shoulder bag. That was what got her into trouble.

Tetley is the loved and pampered pet of Cindy Powers and her husband, Glenn Edwards, who are medical equipment dealers. The little dog went everywhere with them. It went to the theater, to restaurants, even to business meetings. On Saturday afternoon, May 6, 1995, the couple and their 5-year-old son Max were walking down a subway platform. As usual, Tetley was with them, riding in a shoulder bag that Edwards was carrying.

A man riding between subway cars leaned over and tore the bag off Edwards's shoulder. It was a typical bag-snatching. But the thief certainly had no idea what was in the bag.

The couple was distraught. The little dog was a part of the family. They rode the next train all the way to the end of the line to see if there was some sign of the thief or the missing dog. They found nothing.

The next morning Cindy Powers walked into the Jim Dandy Copy Center to get some lost-dog posters printed. She was willing to pay a $1,000 reward, no questions asked, for the return of Tetley.

Hilde Ringel, co-owner of the copy shop, printed the posters and handed out some free advice. She told Powers to get as much press coverage as possible, "because there are a lot of great people in this city who really care about animals."

So the distraught dog owner and the woman from the copy shop began calling all the newspapers, radio stations, and TV newsrooms they could find. A lot of them were interested in the story.

The area in which Tetley was stolen was plastered with reward posters.

"Guys handing out menus on the corners volunteered to hand out our posters," Edwards said.

By that evening, Edwards and a crew of police detectives were on a subway train searching the tracks between 72nd and 96th Streets. "We were in the front car with the door open looking for the bag," Edwards said. "I was worried the dog was going to die in the bag in the tunnel."

There were other worries. Tetley was not a very healthy dog. She needed medicine and a special diet. She often had to be fed by hand.

The media blitz began to pay off. Calls were

Cindy Powers and husband Glenn Edwards are greeted by four-pound Tetley after his safe return. *(AP/Wide World Photo.)*

coming in. Many of the leads, like the one about a chihuahua running wild in Central Park, turned out to be false.

One of the calls, however, sounded very promising. It came from a man who worked in a grocery store. He said his girlfriend had the dog. Early Monday morning, with one of the local TV stations acting as a go-between, Nilda Quezada called Powers. "My wife yelled the dog's name over the phone, and the woman said her tail was wagging and that she was happy," Edwards reported.

Before that, Tetley wasn't happy at all. Quezada said she bought the dog on Saturday at a subway station from a man who wanted $25. "I told him I'd give him $20. I took her home and we gave her milk. We made a little bed for her and bathed her."

On Sunday, Quezada took the little dog to a park in New Jersey. But the dog wasn't happy. "Even when we fed her. Even when we played with her. She did not want to play. She just went to the box and lay down. I felt sad. That's mostly why I called."

The police said that what had happened followed a pattern of bag snatchings from moving subway trains in Manhattan, though this was the first time that a bag contained a dog. According to police, they had a lead to the identity of the dognapper.

Tetley's owners were overjoyed to have their dog back, and at the way people had responded to their pleas.

"People ask me why I love living in New York," Powers said. "It's because there are great people in the city."

5

Out of the Ice

On October 7, 1988, Roy Ahmaogak looked out over the waters of the Arctic Ocean near Barrow, Alaska. He spotted three whales breaching—that is, coming up for air—just offshore.

He immediately knew there was something wrong. Whales are quite common in the Arctic Ocean, but not this kind of whale. Roy recognized these as California gray whales. Bowhead whales may come that far north, but gray whales rarely do. Besides, by October, the gray whales should have already begun their 5,000-mile migration south to warmer waters off the coast of Mexico, where they breed. They spend a lot of time along the California coast. That is why they are called *California* gray whales.

Roy had another thought. The waters of the Arctic were already beginning to ice over. Temperatures were averaging 11 degrees below normal. Winter was coming early. If the whales didn't get out of there and into the open sea fast, they would be trapped. But the whales—all believed to be about 1 or 2 years old—didn't leave. In a matter of days the ice had grown so thick that they were trapped just 100 yards off the coast of Barrow. Miles of ice-covered water separated them from the open sea. And the ice field was growing.

Though they live in the sea, whales are mammals. They must come to the surface to breathe air. If the water in which they swim is covered by a thick coat of ice, they can't get to the surface, and they will soon drown. In the far north, whales have become trapped in the ice, just as these three were. This can happen, particularly when winter comes early. Such incidents rarely attract attention, but this one did, and in a spectacular way.

Out of the Ice

Roy Ahmaogak reported the trapped whales to local wildlife officials. Word got around quickly. In just a few days the story of the three gray whales trapped in the Arctic ice became one of the biggest stories in the world.

As news of the whales' plight spread, reporters began arriving in Barrow. While Barrow, located on Alaska's North Slope, is isolated, it's not all that isolated. Particularly for that part of the world. It is, for example, just 14 miles from the only television station for hundreds of miles. The reporters could send back stories and pictures of the whales' plight almost instantly. Each night on the evening news, people from Alaska to Alabama to Africa were seeing pictures of the whales poking their heads up through the ice hole at Barrow, and hearing accounts of how the ice was closing in on them.

The whales were given names. Biologists called them Bonnet, Crossbeak, and Bone. The names sort of described what the whales' heads looked like. But the Eskimo names—Putu, Siku, and Kanik, or Ice Hole, Ice, and Snowflake— were the names that caught on.

The most immediate problem was keeping the holes in the ice open so that the whales could come up for air. It was clear that they had already injured themselves trying to break through the thickening ice so that they could breathe.

The men of Barrow stood out on the ice, cutting away at the holes with flat-bladed ice choppers. Some were paid minimum wage for the work; many were volunteers. Temperatures fell as low as 10 degrees below zero. The chopping went on around the clock. At that time of year, the nights were 16 hours long in Barrow.

But keeping the holes in the ice open was not a solution. A way had to be found to get the whales back to the open sea. This was going to be a huge job. The open sea was now some 200 miles away. But a break in the ice cap, called a "lead," came within 5 miles of where the whales were trapped. If they could get to the lead before it froze over, they might be saved. The effort to free the trapped whales was dubbed Operation Breakthrough.

The obvious solution to the problem was to have an icebreaker cut through the 5 miles separating the whales from the lead. However, U.S. icebreakers had already left the area, afraid that they would get stuck in the ice.

Within days, the story of the three trapped whales had become so huge that support of one sort or another was pouring in from everywhere. President Ronald Reagan sent a message of encouragement to the rescuers. The oil industry donated equipment and supplies. Even the National Guard supplied two mighty Skycrane helicopters to aid in the effort.

A 193-ton ice-breaking barge had been parked at Prudhoe Bay some 200 miles from Barrow for about 4 years. The barge was dug out of the snow and ice, and dragged by one of the helicopters. It took 3 days to pull the barge a mere 8 miles along the rugged ice field, so the attempt was stopped. Even if the barge could be towed to Barrow, it would be too late.

Rescuers thought about blasting a trail of holes in the ice so that the whales could have places to come up for air on their way to the lead. But they worried that the explosions would damage the whales' sensitive hearing. Then one of the

A member of the rescue team says goodbye to one of the trapped gray whales shortly before the whale headed for open water.

(AP/Wide World Photo.)

Out of the Ice

Skycranes was outfitted with a 10,000-pound concrete cylinder to be used as a battering ram. The cylinder was lifted about 5 feet into the air and dropped onto the ice. In three or four tries it opened an adequate breathing hole.

Despite all the interest and all the efforts, time was running out for the whales. After about a week, one of the whales, Kanik—the smallest—no longer appeared at the ice holes to breathe. Observers assumed that it had drowned beneath the ice.

Still, the effort was not stopped. Finally, help arrived from a most unexpected place. A couple of Russian icebreakers, the *Admiral Makarov* and the *Vladimir Arseniev*, were sent to help in the rescue effort.

The powerful Russian ships were just what was needed. They were able to smash their way through the Arctic ice and cut a channel between the trapped whales and the open lead.

Encouraging the whales to swim in the right direction was painstaking. The spectators cheered as the whales finally swam into the slush-filled channel. One rescuer said, "I feel like my burden is lifted."

There is no way of knowing if Putu and Siku successfully made it to the coast of Mexico to rejoin others of their species. They were exhausted by their ordeal, and the trip would be a long one. But now they had a chance.

After the rescue was over, there were complaints. Some said that because of all of the publicity, the project had gotten completely out of hand. It wasn't the biggest deal in the world. Whales getting trapped in the ice was just part of nature. It happened all the time.

Operation Breakthrough was very expensive. It cost the U.S. over $1 million. And it probably cost the Russians a lot of rubles as well. The money, the critics said, could have been better used somewhere else.

Besides, some people added, all of that time, effort, and money were spent on saving a couple of whales who might not even survive. At the same time whales were still being killed both legally and illegally all over the world.

All of the criticisms were true. But they seemed to miss the point. After centuries of killing whales—after nearly driving many whale species to extinction—people showed that they really cared about these great creatures.

"We thought the phone would stop ringing when they got free, but it hasn't," said Howard Braham, an ecologist who is the director of the National Marine Mammal Laboratory in Seattle, Washington. "People now are asking better questions, looking for perspective. They want to know how the whales are doing. Not just those two, but all the great whales."

In fact, Operation Breakthrough isn't the only sign of the growing human concern for whales. All of the demonstrations and the Save the Whale campaigns have had an effect. Whale hunting has been reduced, if not entirely stopped. And the decline in the number of whales has ended. For a few whale species, like the California gray whale, the numbers have even risen.

6

The Rescue Dog

By tradition, dogs and cats are supposed to be natural enemies. But don't tell that to Ginny the dog. She not only loves cats, she rescues them.

The June 1994 issue of *Good Housekeeping* told the story of Ginny, "an odd mixture of a Siberian husky and a schnauzer."

In 1991, Philip Gonzalez, who lives on Long Island, New York, adopted Ginny from a local shelter. She was about a year old at the time. He just wanted a dog. But this dog had an obsession.

From the start, Ginny showed a particular affection for cats. And she was able to communicate this affection to her new owner. Together, Philip and his dog began feeding stray cats in the neighborhood. Ginny would locate them and Philip would feed them.

It didn't stop there. One day, Philip was driving Ginny past the animal shelter and the dog made so much noise that he decided to take her in for a visit.

During the visit, Ginny seemed to fall in love with a white, blue-eyed cat named Madame. Though Philip had no intention of adopting a cat, he walked out of the place with Madame. As it turned out, this cat was totally deaf. Deafness is common in white, blue-eyed cats. Philip hadn't known that, but he thinks Ginny did.

Another visit to the shelter resulted in the adoption of Revlon, an orange-and-white cat with one eye. Then there was a stray cat named Vogue. After that came a crippled cat named Betty Boop.

Next, Ginny located five kittens in an abandoned building. Philip found homes for two of them and kept the other three.

After about a year, Philip had a houseful of

cats and was feeding about 40 strays. He caught those he could and took them to the veterinarian to be neutered and given their shots. He also tried to find homes for as many as possible. All of this took time and money. Veterinary bills alone ran to several thousand dollars. Somehow, and without making any conscious decision, Philip had become an animal-rescue person. "And it was all because of Ginny," he said.

Philip's house is pretty full of cats now. The animal shelter from which he adopts them has slowed down giving him cats. But every once in a while, Ginny still finds a stray that she likes, and if Philip can't find a home for it, he will take it in to his own crowded house.

"We're just a big, happy family," he says.

7

In Sheep's Clothing

Llamas are a South American relative of the camel. They have long necks and bodies covered with thick wool. Big llamas may stand 6 feet tall. They have dignified, almost stuck-up expressions on their faces. When llamas are happy, they will hum. When they are angry, they will spit. Most people think that these stubborn animals are funny looking. They will not pick fights, but will defend themselves by kicking.

Thousands of years ago, the people of the mountains of South America tamed the llama. It may have been the only tame animal in the Western Hemisphere before the Europeans arrived. Llamas were used mainly as pack animals, to carry heavy loads along steep mountain roads and trails. Their wool was used as the wool of a sheep is used. And sometimes they were eaten.

The llama was never really popular in North America, until recently. But suddenly it seems llamas are turning up in the strangest places, doing the strangest things.

Around 100 years ago, llamas began trickling into the United States. Mostly they were seen in zoos. But some rich people kept them as pets. The newspaper publisher William Randolph Hearst had a herd of them at his California mansion. Michael Jackson now keeps them at his ranch. Ordinary folks have begun raising them as well. No one knows how many llamas there are in the United States, but the International Llama Association has 2,500 American members.

Today llamas are certainly not eaten. Llama wool has a small market, but it has never caught on in the United States. Still, llamas are being put to work at many jobs. The U.S. Forest Service and the National Park Service use llamas to carry equipment on rugged and remote trails. Some

Llamas are used as caddies at North Carolina's Tala-more Golf Course.

(Courtesy of the Talamore Golf Course.)

people think they are better at the job than horses and mules. Llamas have padded feet rather than sharp hooves, and don't damage trails. They are also easier to handle than the average horse or mule.

At the Talamore Golf Course in Southern Pines, North Carolina, llamas are used as caddies. They carry a golfer's clubs from one hole to the next.

But far and away the most unusual use for llamas, and the one that is making the most news, is to guard sheep from predators, particularly coyotes. Llamas look a lot more like something that would be eaten than they do like guard animals. That's why this particular use for the animal is such a surprise.

Over the last 15 years some ranchers began raising llamas to sell to the pet market. Sometimes llamas were kept with sheep. The sheep and llamas got along very well. Ranchers who kept sheep and llamas together found that they lost fewer sheep and lambs to predators.

There has been a lot of discussion about why llamas are such good guard animals. One reason appears to be that the coyote doesn't like anything new. If he meets something unfamiliar, he will run away. A llama is certainly new to most coyotes.

Some ranchers put burros or donkeys with their sheep. Coyotes are not familiar with these animals either, and they seem to stay away. Burros are a lot bigger than coyotes and they make horrible loud noises. Llamas are big too, but they are quiet. And they seem to be even better guard animals.

Though a llama may look like a big, long-necked sheep—and has sometimes been called the sheep of South America—it doesn't act like a sheep. If a llama feels threatened, it will not freeze in fear or run away like a sheep. It will fight back. Some ranchers have reported seeing a llama chase and kick a coyote. There are even stories of llamas killing a coyote.

A llama is no match for a cougar or mountain lion. In parts of the country where these big cats live, llamas cannot be used as guard animals. But the cougar's range is limited. A llama is also no match for a group of coyotes hunting together. But the coyote is usually a solitary hunter.

While larger predators, like the wolf, have been almost eliminated from much of North America, the coyote has not only survived, it has prospered. Coyotes have moved into areas abandoned by other predators. Once thought of as primarily a western animal, the coyote has moved east. They now inhabit every state but Hawaii. Coyotes have even been found living in parks and cemeteries in New York City.

Sheep farmers have waged a relentless war against coyotes. They have been trapped, snared, shot from the air, and poisoned. These methods are cruel, and they haven't worked very well. Of the 500,000 or so sheep that are killed by predators every year, it is estimated that coyotes account for over two-thirds of the kill. Coyotes are more numerous than ever because they have adapted very well.

Usually dogs have been used to guard sheep as well as herd them. A guard dog and a herding dog are very different. A guard dog is usually a large dog that lives with the sheep and can be very fierce. The Great Pyrenees is popular as a guardian of sheep in parts of the United States. Sheepherding dogs are smaller, highly trainable breeds, like the Border Collie. The guard dog is always with the sheep and develops a bond with "his flock." The herding dog lives with humans and follows human commands.

Sheep-guarding dogs can be very good at their job. They have been used for centuries in Europe and parts of Asia. According to C. J. Hadley, the editor of *Range* magazine, "Ranchers say that if a dog bonds with the herd or flock early and develops a protective instinct, and if it doesn't play too hard and injure the sheep and lambs, and if it doesn't get sick or wander, or destroy property, or interfere with a herding dog, or attack humans, or get run over by a car or caught in a coyote trap, then the dog is a good guard."

As you can see, while the dog is a good sheep guardian it has a number of disadvantages. Llama fanciers say their animal makes a better guard. Llamas don't wander off or get into fights, or get hit by cars. They don't get as many diseases as dogs, either. As a result, they live a lot longer than most guard dogs. Llamas can live up to 20 years.

Llamas are more expensive than dogs. A good guard dog costs $300 or $400, while llamas start at $700 and go up—way up. Some llamas cost thousands of dollars. But a llama doesn't have to be trained. Just put it out among the sheep and it knows what to do. Llamas seem to regard sheep as rather dim-witted relatives that need to be protected. Only 40 percent of trained guard dogs turn out to be really good, while 95 percent of llamas are.

Llamas don't need special food. They eat pretty much what the sheep eat—grass. And they aren't greedy. They don't seem to hog the food even though they are bigger than the sheep. Dogs, however, need special food every day.

Llama enthusiasts, of which there are a growing number in the United States, say that the animals are good for more than work. They claim that llamas make excellent pets—or companion animals, as they usually prefer to call them. The llama is too independent to be called a pet.

In Sheep's Clothing

The llama has been described as more like a "long-legged cat, home-loving but independent, treating its owners with affable condescension, thinking up games to play in its spare time, enjoying a challenge, rejoicing in obstacle courses, and learning its assignments only when they look like fun."

And, like cats, they can even be trained to use litter boxes!

8

A Retirement Home for Cats

You must have seen some of those TV ads for retirement homes. An older couple is shown playing golf, swimming, and generally living the good life.

Well, cats don't play golf. And they certainly don't swim if they can help it. A cat's idea of luxury is somewhat different from ours. But cats do have a retirement home. There is a place where aging felines can spend their days in ease, comfort, and safety.

This unique institution is called the Last Post.

A Retirement Home for Cats

It's located deep in the woods of northwest Connecticut, at the end of a winding dirt road.

Perhaps you have been to an animal shelter. There, you've seen dogs and cats kept in kennels or metal cages. No matter how good the shelter may be, it doesn't look like a home.

The Last Post looks like home, because it *is* a home. The feline residents, about 300 of them at any given time, spend their days lounging on couches and easy chairs that are scattered throughout two huge rooms. All the furniture is covered with throws and rugs that are washed daily.

The cats can listen to music if they like. Soft music is usually playing. Whether the cats are actually listening is a matter of opinion. There are exposed beams for climbing or simply for sharpening claws. And there are lots of skylights and bay windows for sunning—a favorite feline occupation, particularly for older cats.

It's the sort of place that cats might design for themselves.

A ground-floor window or door is usually left open so that cats can come and go as they please.

There is a 100-foot sundeck outside, where the cats sun themselves when the weather is nice.

The cats at the Last Post can wander at will through 5 acres of fenced-in fields and woods. While most of the cats choose to divide their time between indoors and out, an independent few have chosen to spend all of their time in the woods. Of course, they always show up at the house for mealtime.

Though there is nothing to stop a cat from running away from the Last Post, the fences are more for keeping other animals out, than keeping the cats in. Anyone who has ever owned a cat knows that a fence will not stop a determined runaway. But at the Last Post there is nothing to run away from. Todd Boibeaux is a manager and one of the full-time staff members of the institution. He told a reporter for *People* magazine, "In my 4½ years here, we've had almost 1,900 cats, and there's only one I can't account for. He just disappeared. To this day, I think someone made off with him."

The Last Post was founded in 1982 by Pegeen Fitzgerald. For many years Pegeen and her husband Ed were well-known New York radio personalities. Their talk show was gentle, particularly when compared with radio talk shows that are popular today. Pegeen was also a passionate animal rights advocate. She regularly supported animal causes on her radio show. Pegeen didn't just talk about animals either. The Fitzgeralds' New York apartment became a regular drop-off spot for pets whose owners had become too old, ill, or unable to care for them. Pegeen and Ed kept some of the animals themselves and found homes for others. But there were just too many animals coming in to be handled that way.

In 1982 Pegeen Fitzgerald bought a 37-acre boys' camp near Falls Village, Connecticut, and turned it into the Last Post. Money to purchase the property came from an animal welfare organization and a foundation set up by Pegeen. To this day, the home is maintained by donations.

In some cases, the cats themselves actually help to support the Last Post. There are a number of "trust fund kitties"—that is, cats who have been left money by their owners. One person who placed a cat in the home left a will of $2 million for the pet.

That's the exception. Most often owners don't even have the $50 that it costs to get the cat through the first few weeks. However, they may donate furniture and bed linens—always useful as replacements in a place where there are 300 cats sharpening their claws.

There is enough space for a lot more cats in the Last Post, but Pegeen always insisted that they should not be overcrowded. If there are too many cats, they can't get away from one another and they begin to fight. At the Last Post, there is nothing to fight about.

Some of the staff members jokingly refer to the Last Post as a "Club Med for Cats" or the "Kingdom of Cats." Even so, when most cats arrive, they have trouble adjusting. From a home where they may have been the solitary center of attention, they suddenly find themselves sharing the limelight with 299 others. But adjust they do, and usually rather quickly.

Staff members try to treat each of the residents as an individual. They pride themselves on knowing the name of each cat. That's no small task when there may be as many as 40 black cats on the grounds. The cats can be told from one another more by personality than by appearance. Every cat acts differently.

The resident with the most unusual history is a large white-and-black cat named Scheherazade, though she is usually called Sherry for short. This cat comes from the Middle Eastern country of Kuwait. After the Gulf War in 1992, the U.S. Army tried to locate and destroy many of the explosive devices left behind by the war.

Lieutenant David Haines, now a student at the University of Connecticut medical school, saw a cat playing with an unexploded dust-colored cluster bomb. Because the cat found the bomb, the soldiers were able to dismantle it harmlessly. Then they wondered how to reward a cat that might have saved their lives. Lieutenant Haines had heard of the Last Post, and suggested that they send Sherry there. And they did. The cat even had her own passport. The desert cat is now a permanent resident of the Connecticut countryside.

Some of the residents of the Last Post sun themselves on the deck.

(Courtesy of the Last Post.)

A Retirement Home for Cats

In some ways, the Last Post serves as a traditional shelter. Most of the cats are up for adoption, unless their previous guardians have requested that they not be adopted. In fact, it is usually hard to find suitable homes for older cats. All cats who are not adopted live out their natural lives at the Last Post.

The Last Post welcomes and encourages visitors. For the cat owners who are still alive but unable to make the trip, there is a speaker telephone that helps them keep in touch with their pets. "We bring the cat into the main office," one of the workers at the sanctuary told *People*, "and hold the phone up to its head."

Though the Last Post was established for cats, a lot of other animals wind up there as well. The sanctuary places over 100 dogs a year in new homes. And there is the occasional pig, sheep, or goat.

And there are still other furry visitors. Raccoons and opossums wander in out of the woods at night to eat the cats' food. The cats don't seem to mind. One worker commented, "For them it's like having friends over for dinner."

9

Sherlock's Home

If a dog is lost or stolen, it's very sad. But when the missing dog is named Sherlock and he is a trained search-and-rescue dog, then it's also a bit embarrassing.

That's just what happened to Sherlock, a 3-year-old golden retriever. Sherlock belonged to Alessandra Eyler, who is a laboratory manager for a company in Oregon.

Sherlock should have been a good name for the dog. He was in training to be a search-and-rescue dog with the Mountain Wilderness Search Dogs. However, unlike the eccentric and often impolite detective after whom he was named,

Sherlock's Home

Sherlock the retriever was pleasant and good-natured and loved everyone. He didn't smoke a pipe or wear a "deerstalker" hunting cap. All he wore was a blue nylon collar.

On Sunday, March 5, 1995, Eyler took her 7-year-old nephew to the Oregon Museum of Science and Industry. She drove her Toyota pickup truck, with Sherlock in the back. Sherlock stayed under the truck's canopy while Eyler and her nephew went inside to see the exhibits.

When they came out, the pickup was gone, and so was Sherlock.

Eyler spent the next day checking with all the animal shelters and veterinarians in the surrounding area. Sherlock was wearing his dog tag, so he could be identified if someone found him. But he had vanished without a trace.

Alessandra Eyler was heartbroken. Losing Sherlock was "the worst thing that's ever happened to me. Take my truck, take everything in it," she said. "But don't take my dog."

Lost-dog stories are all too common. But because of the name of this dog and because he was a trained search-and-rescue dog, this particular story caught the attention of a reporter for the Portland *Oregonian*. The story on the disappearance appeared under the headline MORIARTY DID IT. Professor Moriarty was Sherlock Holmes's archenemy.

The story even made the Internet. News of Sherlock's disappearance was e-mailed to all the Sherlock Holmes fans who are part of the group, Hounds of the Internet. Inevitably, the dog was referred to as Sherlock Hound, though he was really a retriever.

The publicity paid off. On Tuesday the 7th, the missing pickup truck was spotted, and Sherlock was still in it.

Since Monday night, the truck had been left in the parking lot of a school not far from where it had disappeared. It would be nice to say that it was an *elementary* school (you know, "Elementary, my Dear Watson") but it was the Clackamas High School. The school custodian noticed the truck parked in the lot on Monday night, and when it was still there on Tuesday morning, he called the local sheriff.

The sheriff knew that the truck had been

reported stolen, and when he inspected it he found Sherlock under the canopy. The dog was unharmed.

Alessandra Eyler was notified immediately. She said that her dog looked a little depressed, but was otherwise healthy. He was, however, very thirsty. "The vet said give him water and he'll be fine," she told reporters. He drank what was for him a record amount of water.

The police said that there were no suspects in the case. They figured that the truck had been used either for joyriding or as a getaway vehicle. The thieves probably didn't even know that Sherlock was in the back.

The newspaper report on the case concluded: "In the end, despite Eyler's fears and even though he was found at a high school, Sherlock's recovery was elementary."

Now, if only Sherlock was able to live up to his name, those car thieves would really be worried.

10

Humphrey the Wrong-Way Whale

In the fall of 1985 a group or pod of humpback whales was migrating southward along the California coast. They were coming from Alaskan waters where they had spent the summer feeding and storing up fat for the long trip.

On October 10, as the pod passed the entrance to San Francisco Bay, one of the group made a totally unexpected left turn. The whale swam right under the famous Golden Gate Bridge and entered the bay. Humpback whales are rare enough out in the ocean. In San Francisco Bay, they are practically unheard of. In fact, no one could ever remember seeing one there before. Now, there was one.

There are always a small group of people who regularly watch the whales migrate past San Francisco. So this whale's change of direction had not gone unnoticed. But to boaters and others in the bay, the sight of the whale pushing its giant head out of the water was quite startling.

A fully grown humpback whale can be over 60 feet long and weigh more than 100,000 pounds. It looks as big as a bus and weighs more than seven elephants.

The humpback whale is an endangered species. In 1985, there might have been only 10,000 of them in the entire world, and the North Pacific population, to which this particular whale belonged, might have numbered a mere 2,000. Today, the estimated population is slightly larger, particularly in the North Pacific, but the humpback whale is still considered an endangered species.

Humpbacks are probably the most popular of all the great whales. They are good acrobats. Despite their size, they can leap entirely out of the water. They often slap their long flippers against the surface of the water. And when they dive, they wave their tails, or more properly their flukes, in the air. In short, the humpback whale can put on quite a show when it wants to.

In addition, humpbacks are the noisiest of all the whales. The complex and often melodic underwater sounds that they make have been recorded by scientists. These sounds have been called "songs." Scientists believe that the sounds help whales communicate with one another. There is even a popular recording of whale sounds called *Songs of the Humpback Whale.*

So when a member of this very striking and well-known whale species suddenly turned up in San Francisco Bay, it immediately became an object of great interest.

The press quickly named the animal Humphrey the Humpback Whale. He was also called the Wayward Whale, the Lost Whale, or most often, the Wrong-Way Whale.

Biologists determined that Humphrey was a young whale, not yet fully grown. Whales, usu-

Humphrey the whale follows the boat that lured him back to San Francisco Bay.

(Bettmann/UPI/Russ Reed.)

ally young ones, often make what appear to be wrong turns while migrating. No one really knows why. Usually the whales are able to turn around and rejoin the others. And everyone expected Humphrey to do the same. But he didn't.

First he headed south and swam under the Bay Bridge, between San Francisco and Oakland. Then he turned north again and went back under the Bay Bridge. If he had retraced his original path, he would have returned to the ocean, but he kept on swimming north.

He headed into smaller and shallower bays, and finally into the Sacramento River. He was swimming upstream and getting farther and farther from the ocean.

Humphrey was navigating channels that were so narrow and shallow that his flippers were often brushing the bottom. While humpback whales are creatures of the deep ocean, they actually spend a lot of time in fairly shallow southern waters. So they are more accustomed to shallow water than one might imagine. Still, Humphrey was clearly lost, and why he kept swimming in the wrong direction no one could say.

The Wrong-Way Whale was now big news. People lined up on the banks of the river to see him go by and to cheer.

He swam under a drawbridge at Rio Vista. Then he somehow managed to squeeze between a row of pilings that held up an old bridge. He finally came into a spot called Cache Slough—some 70 miles from the open ocean. And it was here that Humphrey the Wrong-Way Whale stopped. The slough, a sort of swamp, was in the middle of a field, and it was so shallow and small that the whale barely had room to turn around.

The scientists who were watching Humphrey knew that he was in big trouble. Whales live in the salt water of the ocean. They can survive in fresh water, for a short while. But the fresh water will ultimately damage their skin and create other health problems. Humphrey had been in fresh water for several days, and he was beginning to look sick. Sores had developed on his skin.

So an effort was launched to get the whale swimming back downstream toward the open ocean. The rescuers tried to use the whale's acute sense of hearing to make him move in the right direction. They collected a fleet of boats. Long metal pipes were lowered from the boats into the water, and then crew members banged on the pipes. This made a horrible noise. It was hoped that the noise would drive Humphrey back downstream.

Unfortunately the whale seemed unwilling to go back through the pilings under the old bridge. So engineers moved in some heavy equipment to enlarge the openings between the poles. That worked, and the whale swam back under the bridge. He nearly got stuck, but he made it.

The next crisis came at the Rio Vista Bridge. It seemed to scare him. Rescuers thought the problem might be the noise from traffic on the bridge. So the traffic was stopped. Behind Humphrey the men in the boats banged on pipes, and the whale went through to the cheers of a large crowd.

Humphrey the Wrong-Way Whale

Once Humphrey passed under the bridge, the rescuers changed their strategy. Instead of driving the whale farther downstream, they now tried to attract him with the recorded sounds of humpback whales feeding. They figured he might be getting hungry. The sounds were played through an underwater speaker on a boat. First the sounds seemed to anger Humphrey. But slowly he began to follow the boat, and as the boat picked up speed, so did Humphrey. He covered 50 miles in a single day. Finally he was back in San Francisco Bay.

Just when it appeared that the whale was going to leave the bay and swim back to the ocean to rejoin the other whales, he stopped and turned around. It looked as if he was getting ready to head back upstream again, this time to certain death.

A call went out for more boats, and soon a whole flotilla was blocking Humphrey's way back. Out toward the ocean were the recorded sounds of other whales. For a while he ignored them. Then he turned and slowly followed them toward the Golden Gate Bridge.

As the now-famous whale passed under the bridge, drivers just stopped their cars to get out and watch. They created an enormous traffic jam, but no one seemed to care. On the shore people were cheering, some even crying with joy.

Humpback whales have very distinctive markings, so it is relatively easy for observers to tell one from another. During his upstream journey, a lot of people got a good look at Humphrey. A few years later, he was spotted, alive and well, passing the Golden Gate Bridge with a group of other whales.

This time he didn't make any wrong turns.

11

Where's Waldo the Whale?

In 1985 when a whale turned the wrong way into San Francisco Bay, and swam upstream, the press called it Humphrey. When the same sort of thing happened on the East Coast almost 10 years later, the press called this whale Waldo the Wrong-Way Right Whale.

This whale appeared in the Delaware Bay early in December 1994. It was identified as a young right whale about 30 feet long. And at first it didn't look as if Waldo had much of a chance of survival. The whale appeared to have been injured, perhaps in a collision with a boat. It was behaving oddly. And there didn't appear to be any way of turning it around to get it back out to sea before it collided with another boat or starved.

The species of this whale made that prospect particularly alarming to biologists. The right whale is probably the most endangered of all the whale species. There may be only 350 of them in the North Atlantic. The loss of even a single individual from this species would be a great loss. Before whale hunting was stopped in the 1950s, the number of right whales had been reduced to as few as 50. The whale got its name because whalers found it so easy to kill. It was the "right whale" to hunt, they said. Now the species is recovering, but very, very slowly. Experts estimate that at the current rate of recovery, it will be another 150 years before the right whale is removed from the endangered species list.

As Waldo made a northward turn and headed up the Delaware River past Wilmington, Delaware, and Philadelphia, Pennsylvania, marine biologists were gloomy. Attempts were made to turn the whale around and to lure it away from the more dangerous portions of the river, where there were more boats. They were only partially successful.

The appearance of the rare whale in the middle of such a well-populated area created a great deal of excitement. In addition to scientists, reporters and photographers were attracted by the whale. And, of course, there were the crowds of ordinary people just hoping to catch a glimpse of the rare creature.

Then, after about 2 weeks of going the wrong way, the whale abruptly turned around and swam back out to sea. Waldo no longer appeared to be injured or sick. Some biologists came up with a new and likely explanation for the whale's journey. He was just exploring.

At one time, before the right whale was nearly exterminated by hunting, they were fairly common along the New Jersey shore. Now they seem to be making a modest comeback. They have been sighted more frequently in the ocean off New Jersey.

Bob Schoelkopf, codirector of the Marine Mammal Stranding Center, says that as whale species begin to recover after the end of whale hunting, more and more whales have begun to move back into the bays and tidal rivers. He thinks they are looking for food.

While Delaware Bay may be a historic feeding ground for right whales, Schoelkopf said it is unusual for them to go as far upriver as Waldo did. However, there are old newspaper accounts of it happening before.

Right whales use both sound and sight to navigate. Waldo may have become confused by the murky water and heavy boat traffic.

Early reports about Waldo indicated that the whale was swimming strangely, with its head out of the water. At first many believed that the whale had something caught on its tail that was unbalancing it. The new theory is that it was just swimming that way in order to see better.

Waldo might not have been lost at all. He might have just been looking around, enjoying the view.

Waldo, a right whale that swam up the Delaware River, spouts water while a nearby police boat watches closely.

(AP/Wide World Photo.)

12

Buddy's Excellent Adventure

It was a great story while it lasted.

On the morning of Sunday, March 12, 1995, Buddy, a 3½-year-old dog, part German shepherd, part mix, wandered off from his home in Central Islip, Long Island, a suburb of New York City.

On Wednesday morning, March 15, a little over 60 hours later, Buddy's owners, the Harrington family, received a call from the Humane Society in Fort Collins, Colorado, some 1,800 miles from Long Island. The Harringtons were told that Buddy had been found wandering near the busy intersection of Riverside and Lemay Avenues in Fort Collins by a woman who brought him to the local animal shelter. Buddy had been identified by his dog tag.

The Harringtons couldn't believe it. "Oh my God. How could he have gotten to Colorado? It can't be the same dog," said Maresa Harrington.

Even a description of the dog didn't completely convince the Harringtons. It all sounded too fantastic. So the Colorado Humane Society officials took four pictures of the dog in their possession and rushed them to New York via overnight mail. Sure enough, it was Buddy.

No one could figure out how Buddy got to Colorado. And at first, no one knew how he was going to get home, either. It is expensive to send a dog from Colorado to New York. But Buddy was lucky once again. The tag he wore came from the North Shore Animal League, a big animal adoption center on Long Island. The North Shore Animal League works closely with one of the largest dog food companies in the world.

The company decided it would be good publicity to help Buddy. Not only would this publicize their dog food, it would give the company the chance to show people the importance of putting identity tags on their dogs. If it had not been for the tag, no one in Fort Collins would have known where Buddy came from. He would have been just another lost dog.

So with his bills being paid by the dog food company, Buddy was loaded onto a Delta Airlines jet at Denver International Airport at 12:50 P.M. on Friday, March 17. About 6 hours later, he arrived at New York's LaGuardia Airport. His disappearance had lasted 6 days. The Harringtons were on hand at the airport for the joyful reunion. So were the reporters and photographers. By this time, Buddy was a celebrity. Not only his picture, but his life story had appeared in the newspapers and on television.

Buddy lived with the Harrington family, Maresa and Pete, and their grown children Brian and Colleen. The dog had been picked out of the North Shore Animal League by Colleen in 1992 as a Father's Day present for Pete Harrington.

Buddy was about 6 months old at the time,

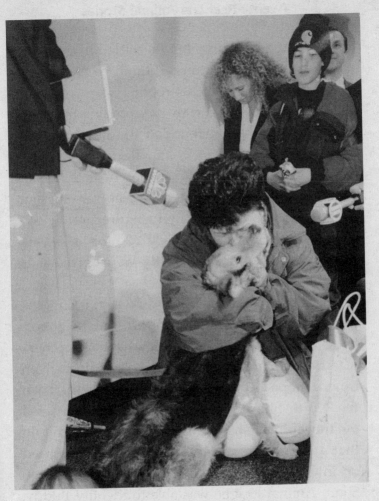

Reporters capture the moment as Maresa Harrington hugs her dog Buddy at New York's LaGuardia Airport after his return from Colorado.

(AP/Wide World Photo.)

and he had a bad lung. But he settled in comfortably with the Harringtons. Though he was Pete's dog, he slept in Colleen's room.

The dog had the run of the family's half-acre property. A fence surrounded the property, but the fence had holes in it, and Buddy wandered out to visit neighbors whenever he felt like it. Maresa Harrington claimed that he rarely went more than two houses in either direction.

Except on Sunday, March 12, for a reason known only to himself, Buddy went farther—as it turned out, much farther.

When they discovered Buddy was missing, the Harringtons frantically searched the neighborhood and contacted local animal shelters. There was no sign of the dog. They had almost given up the hope of ever seeing Buddy again. Then the North Shore Animal League was contacted by the animal shelter in Fort Collins and told that a dog wearing one of their tags had turned up in Colorado. Checking their records, the North Shore Animal League was able to identify Buddy.

The story even got Buddy guest appearances on David Letterman's and Phil Donahue's TV shows.

Buddy's Excellent Adventure

No one could figure out how Buddy got to Colorado. The Harringtons speculated that he could have hopped on a passing truck. They live near a highway and an industrial park. Or perhaps Buddy had been dognapped. No one knew.

Within a few days, the mystery was solved. On March 12, three young men, Joseph VanWart, Robert White, and John O'Brien were driving through Long Island, heading west. They stopped at a gas station in Central Islip, where they spotted a dog nosing through a trash can. It came up with a bagel in its mouth. "We called it over—the next thing we knew it was in the car," VanWart said. "We thought, 'OK, that'll save it from getting hit by a car.'"

And so with the friendly dog aboard, they drove off through New Jersey, Pennsylvania, Maryland, and West Virginia.

Somewhere in the Appalachians, the three stopped for food, and for the first time, took a good look at their canine passenger. That's when they discovered the dog was wearing an identification tag.

"We got worried—we were wondering after

we picked up the dog, did he belong to a little boy," said VanWart. But they were in a hurry and figured they would try to contact Buddy's owners when they reached their destination.

They arrived in Fort Collins on March 14 and stopped at the home of O'Brien's uncle. They let Buddy free. The next morning he was gone again. That's when he was picked up at the intersection of Riverside and Lemay Avenues and brought to the local humane society.

So as it turned out, the mystery of Buddy's disappearance wasn't all that mysterious.

But in the end the important thing was that Buddy got home safely.

"We all just love him to death," Maresa Harrington said. And Buddy, who appeared unimpressed by his brief fame, just seemed happy to be home.

13

First Cat

When Bill Clinton was elected president in 1992, he promised that he would bring change to Washington. Just how much real change he brought and what its effect has been is a subject that will be argued about at great length during the 1996 presidential election.

There is one change that he undoubtedly brought to Washington—Socks the Cat.

Throughout the history of this country, the pet in the White House has been a dog. Some of the presidential dogs, like Franklin Delano Roosevelt's Scottish terrier Falla, Lyndon Johnson's beagles Him and Her, and the Bush family's springer spaniel Millie, became quite famous. A book supposedly written by Millie was a best-seller. (The president's wife, Barbara Bush, really wrote the book.)

The country, however, has now changed. At one time only dogs were considered proper pets. Cats just hung around the house or the barn to catch mice. But then people began taking cats more seriously.

Dogs need a lot of attention, and they need to be walked. In families in which both parents work, and the kids are away at school all day, this isn't convenient. Sometimes it just isn't possible to walk the dog.

A cat can live more comfortably in a small apartment than most dogs. A cat can also exercise itself. Being naturally solitary animals, cats don't get as lonely as most dogs.

The cat seems to be the perfect pet for the modern age, which has been reflected in the statistics of pet ownership. The number of pet cats in the United States is now greater than the number of pet dogs.

So, 1992 was a good time not only for the introduction of a new First Family but for the introduction of a new First Pet—the cat.

Socks captured the imagination and interest of the media, particularly photographers and TV crews. Cats are not very good about giving interviews, so Socks didn't do much radio work. He quickly became the most famous cat in American history.

Socks's origins were humble and a bit mysterious. In November of 1990 he was one of two kittens abandoned on the patio of Nancy Wilcox of Little Rock, Arkansas. She had no idea who left them.

Wilcox had a dog that didn't care for cats. So she put out the word that the kittens were up for adoption. One of her neighbors was piano teacher Anita Reasoner. One of Reasoner's pupils was the daughter of the governor of Arkansas, Bill Clinton. The family dog, a cocker spaniel named Zeke, had just been killed in a car accident. Ten-year-old Chelsea Clinton was heartbroken. When she saw the kittens, she fell in love with them. She was particularly taken with the one with the white toes. That was where the

The Clinton family cat, Socks, gets star treatment from the press after the 1992 presidential election.
(AP/Wide World Photo.)

name Socks came from. The Clintons took the cat to the governor's mansion in Little Rock and ultimately to the White House in Washington.

The second kitten of the pair, an all-black female, was adopted by one of Wilcox's friends, Carolyn Hartstein.

This cat was named Midnight. She is not particularly famous, aside from a brief profile in *People* magazine. She lives the life of an ordinary house cat in Little Rock.

Her owner teases Midnight once in a while by telling her, "You could have been in the White House now, and Socks could have been here with us."

If this bothers Midnight, she hasn't shown her disappointment.

14

Back to the Future with Goats and Camels

Bushes and briar patches can be a big problem for farmers in mountainous areas. The bushes tend to take over the fields. They make it impossible for other types of plants to grow. It's hard to get heavy equipment into such areas to clear the brush. Chemicals to kill the bushes are both expensive and dangerous. And modern technology isn't really much help.

Some agriculture experts are now suggesting

that farmers use a new—or what is really a very old—method of clearing land—goats.

Goats have a reputation for eating just about anything. They are supposed to have a special fondness for eating tin cans. In fact goats don't deliberately eat cans or any other metal objects. The can-eating legend probably started when people saw goats trying to lick the glue from labels on discarded cans.

But the goat's reputation as a hearty eater is well founded. Some historians believe that goats actually ate several civilizations into decline. People in the Middle East kept goats because they were easy to raise, and they required no special care or food. They would just eat whatever was available. They ate plants that cattle and sheep could not digest. And they were such efficient eaters that they could completely destroy a plant. After the goats were finished, there was nothing left to grow back. The goats would then move on.

The result, say the historians, is that the goats would strip an area bare. Then the winds would come and blow the topsoil away. As a result,

Goats like this one are now being used by farmers to clear brush from mountain slopes.

(Bettmann/UPI.)

soil that once grew crops was turned into desert. When agriculture collapsed, civilization went with it.

No one seriously expects goats to destroy the United States. But the agricultural experts do think that the goat's celebrated ability to clear land can be put to good use.

Researchers at the University of Kentucky College of Agriculture and West Virginia University are suggesting that modern farmers do what some ancient farmers did—get a goat, or better yet, several goats.

A series of experiments using cattle, sheep, and goats to clear mountain slopes of brush, blackberry vines, and hawthorn were carried out. The cattle didn't do a very good job. They tended to eat other plants. Sheep did a better job, but they would eat brush only up to the level of their head. Goats, on the other hand, ate it all. They would stand right up on their hind legs and eat everything they could reach.

U.S. government scientists are now looking at an even more exotic animal for the difficult task of clearing brush from pastureland. At least the animal seems exotic to us. It's the camel.

At one time the American Southwest was covered with lush grass. But cattle, sheep, and horses grazed and overgrazed until the grass disappeared. Erosion took away the topsoil, and all that was left was a hard "desert pavement." The land would support only mesquite, creosote bush, tarbush, and broom snakeweed. The names of those plants even make them sound tough and inedible. And for most animals, they are just that.

For a long time now, scientists and ranchers have been trying to bring back the grass. In order to do this, they have to get rid of the tough plants. Mechanical methods are expensive, and don't work very well. Chemical poisons work, but are dangerous. So the U.S. Department of Agriculture (USDA) has decided to try camels.

USDA scientist Dan Anderson says camels have tough mouths, and "they can eat things you wouldn't even want to pick up in your hand."

An experiment in New Mexico using single-

The one-humped camel, or dromedary, has a tough mouth and likes to eat plants that sheep and cattle don't.

(Bettmann/UPI.)

humped camels to clear brush in the Southwest is currently going on. It will take many years to decide if the camels can do the job. But early results are promising. Aside from eating the undesirable plants, the camels seemed to get along quite well with cattle and sheep.

In a sense the reintroduction of camels to the Southwest is like the return of a native. Camels originated in North America. They became extinct here a few million years ago, but they survived in Asia and Africa.

In the middle of the nineteenth century, camels were introduced into the Southwest by the U.S. Army. It was thought they might be used by the cavalry. But that plan didn't work out. There never was a U.S. Camel Corps.

But it's never too late. Maybe someday there will be an Agricultural Camel Brigade.

15

The Great Dolphin Escape

On July 18, 1992, three bottlenose dolphins, Molly, Lady, and Bacall, escaped from the large pen in which they lived at the posh Ocean Reef Club resort in Key Largo, Florida.

Attempts to recapture the trio made headlines across the nation. It also set off an angry debate over whether they should be recaptured.

You may have gone to one of the marine parks like Seaworld, or even to one of the larger zoos, and seen dolphins. Sometimes they are just on display, but often they give shows. Dolphins can be trained to make amazing leaps out of the water, and their shows are very popular.

Dolphins are extremely intelligent animals. They can be very friendly and affectionate to their human trainers. With what appear to be smiles on their faces, captive dolphins always seem happy to us. But are they?

In the ocean, dolphins live in large groups or pods. They swim over a vast area. In captivity, even under the very best conditions, they live a very restricted life. There are many people who think that dolphins should *never* be kept in captivity.

But was freedom right for these particular dolphins? Two of them were well along in years. Molly was 34 and Lady 40. Lady also had a chronic liver condition that required a special diet and medication. They had been in captivity for a long time. There was a real question as to whether they could ever adapt to life in the wild.

Both older dolphins had been captured in the wild and had hard lives in captivity. Both had been part of a traveling animal show. They were transported or sometimes flown from place to place to perform. No one believes that this is a good life for dolphins.

In 1982 Steve McCulloch, who had owned the traveling show, gave up the business and presented Molly and Lady to the private Ocean Reef Club in Florida. They were housed in a lagoon where guests could watch them from a bridge. The trained dolphins regularly gave performances for the guests, who would feed them. The Ocean Reef Club is the last place in America where dolphins are owned privately, and the facility is not open to the public. In 1988, Molly and Lady were joined by two younger and recently captured dolphins called Bacall and Bogie.

The dolphins were supposed to spend the rest of their lives at the club. It was much better than the traveling shows, but it was still a far cry from freedom.

In mid-July, 1992, a lemon shark broke into the dolphins' pen. This seemed to upset them a great deal. Three days later on July 18, Molly, Lady, and Bacall escaped. Bogie stayed behind.

The exact reason for their escape remains a matter of some controversy. They might have broken out on their own after being frightened by the shark, but there was a suspicion that someone deliberately let them out.

The dolphins didn't go very far. They wound up in a 50-foot-by-70-foot, finger-shaped lagoon near the eighteenth hole of a Key Biscayne golf course. It was about thirty-five miles from their home. The older dolphins had been in this particular lagoon before. They had been featured in a made-for-TV movie called *Key Tortuga* that had been filmed there. In many ways it resembled their pool at the Ocean Reef Club.

People who boated on the lagoon loved having the dolphins in their midst. Passersby regularly tossed them fish. At 10 A.M. and 2 P.M.— their normal feeding schedule at Ocean Reef— the escaped dolphins would swim over to a nearby marina and perform tricks, while boaters tossed them food.

Life in this semifreedom was not so very different from life in captivity. The dolphins seemed to be enjoying themselves.

The Great Dolphin Escape

But the owners of the Ocean Reef Club wanted their dolphins back. And they insisted that the dolphins would be safer in captivity. Life in the wild, they said, could be brutal.

Captive dolphins have often been returned to the ocean. The two older dolphins, however, were not good candidates for being returned, particularly Lady, with her chronic liver condition. Besides, dolphins have to be trained to return to the wild and live with other wild dolphins. Bacall might have been healthy enough, but she had not been trained for life in the wild.

These arguments did not impress most animal rights activists. But what really caused problems was the way in which the dolphins were to be recaptured. At first it was hoped that the trio could be lured back with food. But dolphins are clever. They took the food, but refused to follow those who were trying to lure them back.

Days and then weeks went by. In the meantime, the crowds watching the dolphins grew. Reporters and TV crews from all over the country showed up to watch and record the dolphins' antics as they avoided their would-be captors. It was deeply embarrassing for the Ocean Reef Club. All the while, the cry to let the dolphins remain free grew louder and more persistent. It certainly appeared as if the dolphins didn't want to be recaptured. Throughout the country people were rooting for them.

Then the Ocean Reef Club tried to end the drama quickly by catching the dolphins in nets. That really upset a lot of people. Luring dolphins with food is one thing. Physically trapping them in a net and hauling them out of the water while they thrash about is something else. It looks really bad and brutal.

A French diver who watched the netters called the performance "Disgusting. For a country that talks about freedom, these animals chose themselves to be free, and now they're returning them back to jail."

Animal activist Greg Bossart called the operation "a mugging."

Even worse, from the Ocean Reef Club's point of view, was that they still couldn't catch the dolphins. The dolphins would just jump out of the nets as the crowd cheered and the TV cameras rolled.

Tempers were getting short. One animal activist was arrested and was taken off shouting, "If they catch that old dolphin [Lady] they're probably going to kill it."

A dolphin trainer who had been hired to help capture the dolphins became so upset and outraged that he pushed the president of the Ocean Reef Club overboard and was arrested. The TV cameras caught it all. "Those people don't need, don't want, and don't deserve dolphins," he shouted.

In the end, however, the three dolphins were recaptured at night when the cameras were not around. Bacall, the youngest, was the first to be netted. Lady, the crafty old dolphin, kept leaping free of the nets until August 7. She was the last to be taken.

Lady, Molly, and Bacall were unhurt by the netting and seemed unaffected by their brief freedom. After their return to the Ocean Reef Club, they took up life pretty much as it had been before. And they were lucky too. One year later, Hurricane Andrew swept the area and severely damaged the property at the club. But it didn't harm the dolphins.

This highly emotional and well-publicized drama raised a lot of questions about our relationship to dolphins. Is it really right to keep these animals in captivity, no matter how much we enjoy watching them up close? There are no easy answers to this question.

16

The Woodpecker and the Space Shuttle

The launch of the space shuttle *Discovery* was delayed for several weeks in the summer of 1995. The delay was not caused by some difficult technical problem. It was caused by a bunch of male woodpeckers showing off for their mates.

It seems that during the mating season the yellow-shafted flicker, a common woodpecker in the eastern United States, has an odd courtship ritual. The male woodpeckers stake out their territory by making noise. With their strong beaks, they hammer on dead tree limbs. They even hammer on tin roofs. Their aim is to make a great deal of noise: The more noise they make, the more attractive the males are to the females.

Normally this behavior doesn't cause any trouble. But in late May, a group of woodpeckers at the Kennedy Space Center at Cape Canaveral, Florida, decided to take on something a lot bigger than a dead tree. They attacked the space shuttle *Discovery*, which was on the launch pad being readied for an early June launch.

The birds didn't hammer away at the metal skin of the vehicle or the rockets. Even if they had, they wouldn't have done any damage. The woodpeckers attacked a part of the fuel tank that is covered with orange-colored plastic foam. The foam, which is 1 to 2 inches thick, stops ice from forming on the tank when it is being filled with supercold fuels, liquid hydrogen, and liquid oxygen.

The birds pecked about six dozen holes in the insulation, some as big as 4 inches across. In some cases, they hammered right through to the metal.

Engineers examined the holes and decided

they had to be repaired before the shuttle could fly. The repairs were relatively easy. All they had to do was cut out the damaged foam and replace it with a new piece of foam. But the workmen were unable to reach all of the damaged foam while the shuttle was on the launch pad. There was also a worry that the humidity would create problems in patching the foam. So the $2 billion shuttle, built to withstand the challenges of being blasted into space, had been stopped by a bunch of lovesick birds.

Once off the pad and back in the hangar, the repairs took only about a week to make. But then the shuttle *Discovery* ran into scheduling problems, which delayed the launch even more. There was no guess as to how much this delay would cost NASA.

NASA spokesmen tried not to sound too upset over the delay. "I consider this just one more rock in the road to success," said Al Sofage, the assistant launch director.

Could the problem happen again in the future? No one could say. The woodpeckers have always lived around the Kennedy Center. There

A woodpecker pecks holes in the foam insulation of the space shuttle *Discovery,* causing a five-week delay in the launching of the craft.

(Bettmann/UPI.)

had been minor problems in the past. But for some reason, the woodpeckers were more active than usual during the 1995 mating season.

In an attempt to protect the shuttle *Atlantis*, which was also on the launch pad, NASA technicians set up plastic models of owls and played recordings of owls hooting. Owls eat woodpeckers. That seemed to drive the yellow-shafted flickers away, at least for the moment.

No one knows if the woodpeckers will still be fooled by plastic owls and recorded hoots next year.

17

"Yuppie Puppy"

There are gourmet shops for dogs, designer clothes for dogs, motels for dogs, and even summer camps where city dogs can go with their owners for some fresh air. So day care for dogs had to come next.

The Yuppie Puppy Day Care center in Union Lake, Michigan, is where upscale dogs from two-income families come to spend the day while "Mom" and "Pop" are away at work.

Yuppie Puppy is not an old-fashioned kennel where dogs get stuck away in cages for hours. There are cages, of course. But the dogs at Yuppie Puppy spend a lot of time during the average day in play groups with other dogs.

Yuppie Puppy is the creation of Barbara Bocci, a dog trainer and owner of a standard-dog obedience school called Trainer's Academy.

The day-care center is furnished more like a nursery school than a kennel. The place is loaded with rubber balls, squeaky toys, and all sorts of other objects that dogs like to chew and chase. There are even some plastic tunnels for the dogs to crawl through.

Despite the cute name, Yuppie Puppy isn't only for puppies. The "pupils" range from pups just a few weeks old to elderly dogs. But it's the puppies that require the most attention, because they have the most energy. Older dogs are often content to just sit or sleep.

"The puppies have a riot in [the plastic tunnels]," Susan Carpenter, an employee, told a reporter for *People* magazine. "They burn up energy, so when their parents"—the Yuppie Puppy word for dog owners—"pick them up, they're not maniacs."

Dogs are dropped off in the morning, often as

early as 7 A.M., and they are picked up in the evening, usually before 6 P.M. Most dogs adjust easily and happily to the day-care center routine. But there are always those who just don't get along with the other "kids." Some of them even get aggressive and will fight.

For these "problem children," there are special individual sessions of behavioral counseling—or to put it more accurately, private obedience lessons.

But there is no "spare the rod and spoil the child" philosophy here. The training is done strictly by repetition and reward. None of the dogs get hit with a rolled-up newspaper.

Bocci believes that this kind of doggy day care will become common throughout the United States. "The only people who don't understand," she says, "are nonpet people."

18

The Fat Cat

Panther, 13-year-old Carolyn Monroe's 8-year-old cat, had a weight problem. She had eaten her way to a hefty 14 pounds, well above what is considered a healthy weight for a cat of her size and age. The black cat, whose fur has orange flecks, had been put on diet cat food to slim her down. But the diet wasn't working that well, and the weight had not come off. As it turned out, that was a good thing. It probably saved Panther's life.

In March 1995, Carolyn and her mother Linda Monroe were moving from Florida all the way across the country to Portland, Oregon. That's just about as far as you can go in the continental United States.

The movers came into the Monroes' Florida home and began packing things away in boxes. There was a lot of confusion, as there always is in moving.

At some point, while the movers were doing their job, Panther disappeared. Carolyn and her mother checked around the house to see if the cat had run out. Panther couldn't be found. Usually she didn't wander very far.

Carolyn whistled and whistled. That was a sound that the cat normally responded to and came running. But not this time.

Linda Monroe called the movers. Perhaps in the confusion, Panther had gotten inside the van. The movers checked, but found and heard nothing.

The van left Florida for the long trip to Oregon. When it arrived, the Monroe possessions were loaded into a storage locker.

Even then Linda Monroe refused to give up the search for the missing cat. "I'd even been to the storage locker to check, and I didn't hear a thing," she said.

But then one day the movers heard a faint noise coming from the storage locker. When Linda heard it, too, she knew what it was. The movers began taking the boxes out of the locker while Linda whistled. And from one of the last boxes to be examined came an answering "meow."

Panther, limp and exhausted, but possessing just enough strength to meow, was found inside a box that had been stored at the very back of the locker. She had probably become frightened or confused during all of the packing and moving. She must have hidden in a packing box, and was then sealed in by a mover who didn't have the faintest notion that she was there.

Twenty-seven days had passed since Panther had disappeared.

Why hadn't the cat made noises sooner? Why hadn't she responded to the familiar whistle? No one can say. A dog would have barked and whined and made its presence known. But as anyone who has ever lived with a cat realizes, they can be very strange sometimes.

Linda pulled Panther out of the box, covered

Panther was the center of attention as Linda Monroe (*left*) and her daughter Carolyn recovered the cat after she had spent twenty-seven days trapped in a moving box.

(*Joel C. Davis*/The Oregonian.)

her, and rushed her to the office of veterinarian Lynn Erdman. The cat was badly dehydrated but had survived for almost a month packed in a box without water, food, or light. The vet started giving Panther fluids, and by later that day, the cat began cautiously eating her first meal in nearly a month.

"It's just amazing," said veterinarian Erdman. "With cats, they just have a knack to survive."

One of the reasons Panther survived may have been that she had a lot of extra fat. She dropped from a chubby 14 pounds to a skinny 9 pounds as the result of her ordeal.

Carolyn had almost given up hope before Panther was found.

"My mom called me and said, 'I just heard a meow,'" she told a reporter for the Portland *Oregonian*. "I just burst into tears."

19

Successful Return

In early April 1994, a commercial fishing vessel spotted a pilot whale about 20 miles off the New Jersey coast. That was really not much of a story. Like all whale species, the pilot whale has been threatened by whale hunting. But this medium-size toothed whale is still fairly numerous.

What made this whale unusual was that it had a box attached to its dorsal fin.

The sighting was reported to the Okenos Ocean Research Foundation in Hampton Bays, Long Island. They were delighted to hear about it. They knew this whale personally. "Not many whales would fit that description," said Sam Sadove of the foundation.

One thing that pilot whales are known for is beaching, or stranding themselves.

You will often hear of a group of whales that has become stranded on a beach somewhere. These are usually pilot whales. No one knows why it happens. Efforts to save the stranded whales by returning them to the sea are not always successful.

Often the whales are sick or too badly injured to survive after being returned to the water. But sometimes, apparently healthy whales will swim right back on shore. Once again, no one knows why.

In late August of 1993, a young pilot whale was discovered stranded in the shallows of Long Island Sound. Whale strandings in New York tend to get a lot of publicity. She (for the whale turned out to be female) was taken to the New York Aquarium for treatment.

When the veterinarians examined the whale they found that she was suffering from bacterial pneumonia. This was one sick whale, and her chances of survival did not look good.

But the veterinarians treated her with antibiotics and a great deal of tender loving care. Her health care reportedly cost $250,000. Eventually, she recovered. However, the aquarium had no facilities—and no desire—to keep anything as large as a pilot whale. So the decision was made to return the whale to the sea and hope for the best.

In April 1994, some 8 months after she had been found, the 1,100-pound whale was placed in a sling, lifted out of the aquarium tank, and lowered into a padded box on a flatbed truck, and driven to a pier in Brooklyn.

At the pier the box was lifted onto the deck of a Coast Guard ship, which immediately headed out to sea. By early afternoon, the whale was lowered into the Atlantic Ocean about thirty-five miles southeast of Fire Island Inlet. A transmitter in a box was fastened to the whale's dorsal fin. Scientists hoped that the transmitter would help them keep track of the whale's progress.

The whole operation went very smoothly. It took about 11 hours, a fact that pleased the project organizers. The longer a whale is out of the water, the greater the chance of injury or even death. Still, returning a whale to the sea this way is always risky.

That's why sighting the whale off the New Jersey coast a few days later came as such a relief to those who had organized the project.

Now you may ask why they were actually happy to see the whale when she was carrying a transmitter.

The fact is that transmitters don't work very well on whales. In fact, they don't work at all when the whale is underwater, which is most of the time. The signals can be obscured by high waves, weather conditions, and lots of other things. And they often just break down in the harsh environment of the sea.

In this case the transmitter worked, in a way. It allowed a particular whale to be identified.

20

The Nonpolitical Newt

Newts are small amphibians. They rarely attract attention.

Then in 1995 Newt Gingrich became Speaker of the U.S. House of Representatives, and one of the most outspoken political figures in America. Suddenly newts became famous. There were all sorts of articles about what newts were and what they do. And there were the inevitable newt jokes.

Here's one: "What's a newt?"

"Nothing. What's a newt with you?"

All of a sudden newt interest came to the attention of members of the Wodehouse Society. The society is a group of fans of the

126

The Nonpolitical Newt

British–American humorist P. G. Wodehouse—pronounced *Wood*house.

Newts figure prominently in some of Wodehouse's works. One of the writer's most memorable characters is Gussie Fink-Nottle, the world's foremost newt fancier, who has lived "completely surrounded by newts."

Wodehouse fans saw one of their favorite animals become a political symbol, and they didn't like it. So they decided to "take back the newts."

Members contacted the Philadelphia Zoo about sponsoring a newt exhibit. The zoo was absolutely delighted. The zoo encourages people to "adopt" zoo animals—that is, to donate money for the upkeep of certain animals. The zoo is even happier when people donate enough money to actually pay for a new exhibit.

Now, newts are small, and they can be exhibited in a sort of fish tank. So it is not very expensive to build a newt exhibit. But zoo officials pointed out that many species of newts are endangered. They are also the sort of animals that tend to be overlooked at the zoo. People will flock to see the lions or the gorillas. They will barely notice an exhibit of newts or frogs. People don't usually donate money for such animals, either. They thought that such an exhibit would be a wonderful opportunity to publicize "the conservation of these amphibians."

And so it turned out to be. When the exhibit opened in March of 1995, three television crews and an Associated Press photographer showed up.

There they were, all crowded in front of an exhibit that measured only 3 feet by 2 feet by 2 feet, trying to take pictures of creatures that were about 2 inches long, and fairly shy.

No matter. The newt exhibit was shown on all the Philadelphia TV news shows that evening.

Popular Philadelphia *Inquirer* columnist Richard Jones wrote: "Day 65 of the Republican 'Contract With America,' and at the Philadelphia Zoo, it's time for a change.

"The Philadelphia chapter of the Wodehouse Society has teamed up with the zoo to sponsor a new exhibit designed to 'Take Back the Newt.'

"It may seem like a crazy idea, but perhaps there is a confusion of Newts in the world these days."

The Philadelphia Zoo has opened a newt (*above*) exhibit in honor of Gussie Fink-Nottle, the world's foremost fictional newt fancier, a creation of the humorist P. G. Wodehouse.

(Courtesy of the Zoological Society of Philadelphia.)

About the Author

DANIEL COHEN is the author of more than 150 books for both young readers and adults. Though he is best known for his books on ghosts and other supernatural subjects, he has also written many books on animals. His Minstrel titles include *Real Ghosts*, *Phantom Animals*, *The Ghosts of War*, *Phone Call From a Ghost: Strange Tales from Modern America*, and *Ghostly Tales of Love and Revenge*.

Mr. Cohen was born in Chicago and has a degree in journalism from the University of Illinois. Before becoming a full-time writer he was managing editor of *Science Digest* magazine. He has spoken at schools throughout the country and has been a frequent guest on radio and television programs. Mr. Cohen and his wife share a house in Cape May, New Jersey, with two Clumber spaniels and three cats.

DON'T TURN OUT THE LIGHTS
These ghoulish tales will scare you silly!

⟶ GHOSTLY TERRORS ⟵

⟶ THE GHOSTS OF WAR ⟵

⟶ PHONE CALL FROM A GHOST: ⟵
Strange Tales from Modern America

⟶ REAL GHOSTS ⟵

⟶ THE WORLD'S MOST FAMOUS GHOSTS ⟵

⟶ PHANTOM ANIMALS ⟵

⟶ GHOSTLY TALES OF LOVE & ⟵ REVENGE

By Daniel Cohen

Available from Minstrel® Books
Published by Pocket Books

669-02